Yahoo for You

Written by Dana Meachen Rau
Illustrated by Cary Pillo

Reading Advisers:

Gail Saunders-Smith, Ph.D., Reading Specialist

Dr. Linda D. Labbo, Department of Reading Education,
College of Education, The University of Georgia

LEVEL B

A COMPASS POINT
EARLY READER

For Grandma Paula and Grandma Patti

A Note to Parents

As you share this book with your child, you are showing your new reader what reading looks like and sounds like. You can read to your child any-where—in a special area in your home, at the library, on the bus, or in the car. Your child will associate reading with the pleasure of being with you.

This book will introduce your young reader to many of the basic concepts, skills, and vocabulary necessary for successful reading. Talk through the details in each picture before you read. Then read the book to your child. As you read, point to each word, stopping to talk about what the words mean and the pictures show. Your child will begin to link the sounds of the letters with the look of the words that you and he or she read.

After your child is familiar with the story, let him or her read the story alone. Be careful to let the young reader make mistakes and correct them on his or her own. Be sure to praise the young reader's abilities. And, above all, have fun.

Gail Saunders-Smith, Ph.D.
Reading Specialist

Consulting editor: Rebecca McEwen

Compass Point Books
3722 West 50th Street, #115
Minneapolis, MN 55410

Visit Compass Point Books on the Internet at *www.compasspointbooks.com* or e-mail your request to *custserv@compasspointbooks.com*

Library of Congress Cataloging-in-Publication Data
Rau, Dana Meachen, 1971–
    Yahoo for you / written by Dana Meachen Rau ; illustrated by Cary Pillo.
        p. cm. — (Compass Point early reader)
    "Level B."
    Summary: Grandma encourages a fearful child to try new things.
    ISBN 0-7565-0177-6 (hardcover)
    [1. Fear—Fiction. 2. Self-perception—Fiction. 3. Grandmothers—Fiction.] I. Pillo, Cary, ill.
II. Title. III. Series.
    PZ7.R193975 Yah 2002
    [E]—dc21   2001004727

Sometimes I visit
my Grandma Sal.

She always wants me
to try new things.

4

"I don't like to climb," I say.

"Give it a try," she says.

I do. It's fun!

"Yahoo for you!" she says.

"I don't like to swim," I say.

"Give it a try," she says.

I do. It's wet!

"Yahoo for you!" she says.

"I don't like pea soup," I say.

"Give it a try," she says.

I do. It's yummy!

"Yahoo for you!" she says.

"I don't like to ride ponies," I say.

"Give it a try," she says.

I do. It's bouncy!

"Yahoo for you!" she says.

Grandma Sal doesn't always like to try new things.

"I don't like roller coasters,"
she says.

"Give it a try," I say.

She does. She loves it.

"Yahoo for us!" we say.

More Fun Trying New Things!

Are your children sometimes afraid to try new things? Sit down with them and encourage them to list all the things they don't want to try. Then help them think of the reasons why.

After your children make a list, have them help you make a list of your own. Your children will probably be surprised to find that even adults don't always like to try new things.

Then make it a goal to try one new thing each week—either from your lists, or something that just pops up! Perhaps you can visit a new park, read a new book, or swim in the deeper end of the pool.

Trying a new flavor of ice cream can be an adventure. Even if your children don't like it, it is most important that they tried. And trying new things together makes them all the more fun!

Word List

(In this book: 42 words)

a	it	sometimes
always	it's	soup
bouncy	like	swim
climb	loves	things
coasters	me	to
do	new	try
does	pea	us
doesn't	ponies	visit
don't	ride	wants
for	roller	we
fun	Sal	wet
give	say	yahoo
Grandma	says	you
I	she	yummy

About the Author

Dana Rau lives with her family in Farmington, Connecticut, where she writes her books. She loves to try new things. She tried mountain climbing once, and wanted to do it again and again. She didn't think she'd like mangoes, but now they are one of her favorite foods. She is still very scared, though, of going down hills while she's cross-country skiing. Dana's young son Charlie tries new things every day. He tried raisins and loved them—but he still refuses to try applesauce.

About the Illustrator

Cary Pillo loves to draw pictures and swim. Five years ago she decided to swim a race in Lake Washington, a deep, clear lake near her home. She had never done such a thing before. So she practiced swimming in the lake until she was ready. When race day came, Cary was so nervous she had hundreds of butterflies in her stomach! Even though it was scary, she now swims in the same race every year. Cary lives in Seattle, Washington, with her husband Jim, son Seth, and her office buddy, Rocket Dog.